THREE SECRET SEEDS

They were able to make a truly magnificent castle.

THREE SECRET SEEDS

JOYCE REASON

LUTTERWORTH PRESS
LONDON

First published 1964

COPYRIGHT © 1964 LUTTERWORTH PRESS

*Printed in Great Britain by Richard Clay and Company, Ltd.,
Bungay, Suffolk*

Contents

First Seed—Jennifer

PETER, Caroline and Jennifer were batting a ball against the side of the garage, waiting for Mum to come out with the picnic lunch and take them over the sandhills to the sea.

It was not quite holiday time, but they had all had German measles, Jennifer rather badly, so the doctor had said they would be better for a change. Mum had brought them to this little bungalow, which had a quiet road in front and sand-hills behind, and just over the sandhills a lovely sandy shore. There were six bungalows in a row and nobody else in them at all! They had the place all to themselves, because it was only June.

Dad could only come at week-ends, because of business.

Peter and Caroline were twins. They both had round freckled faces and red hair, only Peter's hair was curly and his eyes were brown, while Caroline's hair was straight and she had bright blue eyes. Jennifer was a year younger and much smaller. Her hair was fair and her eyes were grey.

Smack went the ball against the garage wall, and when it bounced back whoever was nearest hit it—smack!—against the wall again. Then Caroline hit it a little too high, and it went up on the roof and stayed there.

"Bother!" said Caroline. "Now what shall we do?"

"It's all right," said Peter. "There's a ladder in the garage. We can easily get the ball down."

He and Caroline brought out the ladder and propped it against the wall. It was just the right height, and Caroline went up it like a squirrel.

"Oh, do be careful!" begged Jennifer. "You might fall!"

Caroline danced on the flat roof. "It's lovely up here!" she sang out. "You can see right over the sandhills to the sea! Do come up, Jen!"

"I'll hold the ladder steady," said Peter. So Jennifer went up, slowly, holding on very tight, and when she got to the top Caroline took her hand so that she wouldn't be frightened. It *was* lovely to see the blue sea with little white waves on it, and the shiny wet sands stretching for miles.

"Why doesn't Peter come up?" Caroline wondered. "Pe-ter!"

The only answer was a laugh. When the girls looked down, there was Peter on the ground, grinning at them, and the ladder wasn't there! He had taken it away.

Jennifer sat down on the roof and began to cry; but Caroline flew into a rage. She gave a great jump off the roof and landed nearly on top of Peter. It was a wonder she didn't sprain her ankle. Then she flew at Peter, punching him with her fists and kicking his shins so that they both tumbled over together and rolled on the ground. Jennifer cried harder than ever.

Mum came out of the bungalow with the picnic basket in one hand and the Blob, their baby brother, perched on her arm.

"Whatever is the matter now?" she exclaimed. "Peter and Caroline, stop

The ladder wasn't there!

fighting at once! Get up, both of you!"

The twins stopped fighting and stood up, all covered with dust. Caroline's knee was grazed and Peter had a scratch all down one cheek.

Mum put the Blob and the basket on the ground and reached up her hands to Jennifer. "Come, darling," she said. "Mum will catch you." Jennifer slid off the roof into Mum's arms and clung to her, still sobbing.

"Now," said Mum to Peter and Caroline, "tell me what it's all about."

"It was Peter," began Caroline, but Mum stopped her.

"Don't tell tales," she said. "Peter, what happened?"

"The girls went up on the roof to get the ball, and I took the ladder away," said Peter sulkily. "It was only a joke. I was going to put it back."

"It was a very silly joke," Mum told

him. "You knew it would frighten Jennifer. I suppose Caroline jumped off the roof—she might have hurt herself badly."

"I didn't think," mumbled Peter.

"That's the trouble," said Mum. "You are too fond of playing tricks, and you don't think what will happen. One day you might do something really dangerous. *Do* try to think, old man!"

"I'm sorry," said Peter. "I *will* try!" And he meant it.

"Caroline," Mum went on, "I don't like these dreadful tempers of yours! Suppose you had jumped right on top of Peter! You might have broken his arm."

"I am most awfully sorry, Peter," said Caroline. "Did I hurt you very much?" She was very fond of Peter.

"No, hardly at all," said Peter stoutly. He was very fond of Caroline.

"I might have." Caroline shook her head. "I *will* try not to lose my temper." And *she* meant it, too!

Mum put her arm round Jennifer. "And Jennifer," she said gently, "I do wish you would try not to cry so easily. I don't want my little girl to be a coward."

Jennifer didn't say anything. She thought to herself, "I don't see how I can keep myself from being frightened. I'm just not brave like Peter and Caroline."

"Well now," said Mum cheerfully, "that's all over, and we'll go and have our picnic. Bless me, where's the Blob?"

The Blob couldn't walk yet, but he could crawl, quick as a little scuttling crab. While they had been talking he had started off on his hands and knees, down the path towards the road. Mum ran after him and picked him up.

"It's no use telling *you* not to do anything!" she laughed. The Blob gurgled and grabbed her hair with his little fat hands. Then they all went over the sandhills to the sea.

He could crawl, quick as a little
scuttling crab

Peter and Caroline soon forgot their
adventure, but Jennifer was very quiet.
She was so ashamed of herself for being
easily frightened, but she didn't know
what to do about it. It was not until
bedtime, when she knelt down to say her
prayers, that a thought came to her.

"I could ask Jesus to help me. Perhaps He would make me brave."

So she put an extra sentence on to her prayer, after "God bless Mum and Dad and Peter and Caroline and the Blob." She said, "And *please, please* make me a brave girl. For Jesus' sake. Amen."

CHAPTER
2

Jennifer and the Blob

FOR several nights Jennifer prayed her prayer, but she did not seem to get any braver. She was still afraid to go out to the edge of the sea, like Peter and Caroline, and splash about in the little waves. The sea looked so big! She preferred to stay in the long pool which the sea left when it went right out, and play with the Blob. It was a beautiful pool, only deep enough to come half way up her legs at one end, and just a few inches at the other. Beyond it the sand made a low bank. But when the tide was high the water came right up to the dry sandy strip under the dunes.

Peter had a little boat with sails, and the pool was just right for sailing it. On the sea the waves kept turning it over, but on the pool the wind blew it across to the other side, and Peter would run round and fetch it and bring it back to sail across again. Caroline and Jennifer watched him for a while, and then went off to gather shells. Mum sat on a rug with her knitting, and the Blob burrowed in the dry sand by her side.

It was a marvellous place for shells. There were shells like tiny snails, yellow and orange and brown; pink shells like butterflies with their wings open, pointy white shells, purple mussels with mother-of-pearl insides, and long narrow shells that Mum told them were called razor

The children kept on finding new kinds

shells. The children kept on finding new kinds.

"Ow!" cried Caroline suddenly, "I've cut my foot on something. It's bleeding."

She had trodden on a broken razor shell.

Caroline hopped. "Mum! Mum!" she called. "I've cut my foot!"

Mum came running. She looked at the cut. "Poor old lady!" she said. "It's only a little cut, but we must get the sand out of it and put on a bit of sticking plaster to keep it clean. I'll give you a piggy-back to the bungalow." She took Caroline on her back.

"Keep an eye on the Blob, Peter," she said. "I shan't be long."

"All right," Peter answered. He looked at the Blob, who was quite happy playing in the sand. Then he went on sailing his boat.

Jennifer wandered on a little way, looking for more shells and thinking how brave Caroline was not to make a fuss.

Peter went on sailing his boat. Presently he forgot to look at the Blob.

The Blob began to crawl. He crawled right down to the shallow end of the pool, and splashed through it. Peter was

at the other end and didn't notice. The
Blob began to scramble up the bank of
sand beyond the pool.

Jennifer filled her pail full of shells.
She saw that she had come quite a long
way along the shore, so she turned and
began to walk back. When she came to
where Mum had been sitting, the Blob
was nowhere to be seen!

Jennifer looked all round. There was
Peter, busy with his boat. The pool had
got much deeper and longer, for the tide
was coming in. Wherever was the Blob?

Then Jennifer saw him, sitting on top
of the sand bank. But oh dear, oh dear,
the sand bank was an island now. The
sea had come right round it, and made a
stream between her and the Blob, and it
was getting deeper fast.

Jennifer saw that there was no time to
call Peter. In a few minutes the water
would be over the bank where the Blob
was. She ran straight into the water.

It *was* deep! It came above her knees, and was hard to wade through. When she got to the Blob he didn't want to come. He wriggled and kicked with his legs, and he was heavy for a little girl of seven to lift. By the time Jennifer got him up in her arms the water was touching their toes.

Now she was badly frightened. Suppose she couldn't get back to the land? But she knew she must get back somehow, so into the water she went. It was really deep now, above her waist, and it pushed against her so that she was afraid she would fall in—and then what would happen to the Blob? The baby thought it was fun, and bounced about in her arms so that she nearly dropped him.

"I can't do it," Jennifer thought. Then she remembered. "Jesus!" she prayed, "please help me!"

She struggled on. Just as she came to

"I can't do it," Jennifer thought

the deepest part she heard Mum's voice.
"Hold on, darling, I'm coming!"

In a second Mum's arms were round
her, warm and strong, and she and the
Blob were lifted through the water and
on to the dry sand. Mum hugged Jennifer hard.

"My brave little girl!" she said. "My
dear, brave little girl!"

"I don't think I was brave," said

Jennifer, trying not to cry now it was all over. "I was awfully frightened! But Mum, I asked Jesus to help me and He did! He made me able to do it!"

"I *am* glad," said Mum. "Now we must get you and the Blob into dry clothes—and I must change my skirt."

Caroline was sitting on the rug. She didn't get up because her foot was still sore, but she clapped her hands as Jennifer passed her.

Mum didn't say anything to Peter. He followed them slowly with his head hanging.

"Mum," said Jennifer while she was changing her clothes, "I don't understand. I asked Jesus to make me brave, but I went on being frightened."

"He made you brave when you had to save the Blob," said Mum.

"But I want to be brave all the time," said Jennifer.

"It's like this," Mum explained. "You

asked to be brave, and Jesus planted a little seed of courage in your heart. You know seeds don't start to grow all at once."

"I know," agreed Jennifer. "They have to be watered."

"That's right," said Mum. "You keep on watering the seed with your prayers, and it will grow."

"I see," Jennifer nodded. "It's my secret seed, Mum."

3

Second Seed — Peter

PETER felt dreadful. Mum didn't scold him, or even ask what had happened. She didn't need to, for she had come over the sandhills just as Jennifer got to the Blob. Peter almost wished she *would* scold.

He went straight to his own little room, which was next to the girls' room, and lay down flat on his bed with his head on his arms.

"I didn't think!" he moaned to himself. "The Blob might have been drowned because I didn't think! I promised Mum to remember, and then I forgot. How does one remember not to forget?"

The walls of the bungalow were thin, and he could hear what Mum and Jennifer were saying about the secret seed and how to water it by praying.

"If Jesus could make Jennifer brave," he thought, "perhaps He would make me remember."

He got off the bed and knelt down. "Please Jesus," he prayed, "plant a seed of remembering in my heart! Do help me to think before I do things! I can't do it by myself. I need You."

After that he didn't feel quite so wretched. He knew he had a kind, strong Friend.

The next day a big car drew up at the bungalow farthest away from theirs. It had piles of luggage on top, and on a trailer behind it a beautiful shiny motor-boat! Out of the car got a young-looking man and woman and a boy about the same age as Peter and Caroline.

"I say!" said Caroline, "they have

The next day a big car drew up

got a lot of things. I expect they're
rich."

"I wonder if the boy would play with
us?" said Peter.

"I daresay he would like to. He seems
to be the only one. When they have
settled down you might go and ask him,"
suggested Mum.

Jennifer didn't say anything. She was

scared of boys—except Peter, of course. "But if he's lonely, I must be nice to him," she told herself. Then she gave a little jump. "I do believe the seed's growing," she thought.

It was the boy who came to them first. When they were all on the sands they saw him wandering slowly towards them. Peter ran to meet him. "Hullo!" he called.

"Hullo!" said the boy.

"I'm Peter."

"I'm Harold. My mum and dad are unpacking. They told me to go and play, but there's nothing to do here."

"Come and play with us," said Peter.

"All right," said Harold, but he didn't sound very keen. "I think this is a dull place."

As they walked towards the others Harold began to boast. "My dad's got a motor-boat. It goes ever so fast."

"Yes," said Peter. "I saw it."

"I've got a boat, too," went on Harold.

"So have I," said Peter. "With sails."

"I mean a real boat," said Harold. "It's a rubber boat that you blow up, and it floats. It has a paddle. I'm going to sail in it. You can come too, if you like."

"That would be fine," said Peter, getting excited.

Caroline came to meet them. Her foot was nearly well. Jennifer followed more slowly. Peter introduced them.

"Now there's four of us, we can make an enormous sand-castle," cried Caroline. Harold stuck his hands in his pockets and looked sulky.

"Building sand-castles is sissy!" he declared.

Caroline's eyes began to sparkle, and Jennifer was afraid she was going to have one of her tempers.

"There are all sorts of lovely shells on

"Building sand-castles is sissy!"

the sand," she said quickly. "We could collect some."

"Shells are sissy!" said Harold.

Peter decided that he didn't like Harold very much, but he remembered that rubber boat, and didn't want to quarrel.

"Well, let's go and sail my boat," he suggested. He wondered if Harold would say that was sissy too, and was a little surprised when the boy answered, "All right, let's."

The two boys went off to the pool. Caroline stamped her foot.

"What a horrid rude boy!" she cried.

"Perhaps he isn't happy," said Jennifer.

"I think he's spoiled," Caroline declared. "Never mind, Jen, we don't want him. We'll build a splendigorgeous sand-castle all by ourselves."

And they did.

4

Peter and Harold

NEXT day Harold came with a polite little note from his mother. She asked if Harold might come and play with the children that afternoon, as she and his father wanted to take some friends out in the motor-boat, and there wouldn't be room for him. Of course Mum said yes, though nobody wanted Harold much. But when he turned up after lunch, bringing a nice cake for tea, they all did their best to be friendly.

Almost at once Harold said to Peter, "My rubber boat's all ready now. Like to come and see it?"

Caroline nearly asked, "Can we come too?" But it was so plain that Harold didn't want the girls that she said nothing. The two boys went along the sand to the end bungalow.

There was the rubber boat, all blown up, with a little paddle in it.

There was the rubber boat, all blown up

"Ooh!" cried Peter, "isn't she grand!"

Harold looked pleased. "Like to have a sail in her?"

Peter was just going to answer "Rather!" when a little voice inside him seemed to whisper, "Stop. Think." He did stop and think. And he remembered that there were some questions he ought to ask.

"Do your mum and dad let you sail her when they're not with you?"

" 'Course they do," said Harold scornfully. "I've often gone in her all by myself."

"On the sea?" asked Peter.

"No, on the lake near our home. What's the difference?"

Peter looked at the sea. It was not quite so fine to-day; there were clouds, and the wind was making tossy little waves.

"I should think," he said, "there's a good deal of difference. I believe we ought to ask my mum first."

"You're afraid!" cried Harold.

"I'm *not* afraid!" Peter shouted. Then he said more quietly, "We should look pretty silly if we upset."

"We shan't upset. This kind of boat doesn't. Come along if you're coming, cowardy custard."

Peter wanted badly to sail in that boat, but he said firmly, "I'm going to ask Mum."

"I shan't wait for you," said Harold, and he pushed the boat (it was very light) into the water and scrambled in. Peter watched. It was pretty to see the way the little boat bobbed over the waves. Harold paddled cleverly.

"See!" he called. "It's easy!"

He paddled away from the shore, and Peter stood still, wishing he was with him. Soon the boat was quite a long way out.

"Now will you come?" Harold shouted, and Peter called "Yes!"

Harold turned the boat and began to

paddle towards the shore. But he didn't seem to get any nearer! In fact he was getting farther away.

"I can't make her go!"

"I can't make her go! I can't make her go!" Harold's voice sounded frightened.

Peter saw that he was drifting out to sea. The tide was going out and he had got caught in a current!

"I'll go and get help!" Peter yelled as loudly as he could, and he ran fast, fast, back to Mum. He was quite out of breath when he reached her.

"Mum! Harold!" he panted. "Boat —out to sea——"

Mum jumped up. She could see the little red boat tossing on the waves, and she guessed what had happened. She ran to the bungalow and telephoned to the lifeboat station. It was only a few miles off.

"They're sending out a boat at once," she comforted Peter when she came back. "They'll soon find him. Those rubber boats are very safe." But she looked worried all the same.

Waiting was rather horrid. Harold's little boat drifted out of sight. The sky got cloudier and the wind blew harder. Then the rain came, and Mum hurried them into the bungalow. Jennifer couldn't help crying when she saw the cake Harold had brought sitting on the table.

"Could we pray for him?" she asked.

"That's the best thing we could do," agreed Mum, and they all prayed for a little boy all alone on a stormy sea.

It seemed such a long while before the telephone rang, and Mum hurried to answer it. "Yes? Yes!" they heard her say. "Oh, good! That's right." She turned to the children.

"They've got him—he's quite safe," she cried, all smiles. "They're bringing him home in a car. Oh, thank God they found him before his mother and father got back!"

Harold came back in a car with a policeman! He was a kind, jolly policeman, but Harold was pale and very quiet. When the policeman had driven away Harold said:

"I'm sorry I called you a coward, Peter. You were quite right—the sea isn't the same as a lake."

"That's all right," said Peter.

"I tell you what," went on Harold, "I'll ask my dad to take us out in his motor-boat—and the girls too, if they like."

"That would be jolly," said Mum. "And now I think we all want some tea, and a slice of Harold's lovely cake."

"Your mum is a decent sort," Harold whispered to Peter. "She hasn't said a word of scolding!"

"She knows how you feel," Peter whispered back.

After tea Mum went with Harold to his bungalow to explain what had happened. Peter put on his raincoat and went to meet her as she came back.

"I wanted to talk to you, Mum," he said. "I very nearly did go with Harold. But—I've been doing like Jennifer and asking Jesus to help me remember, and He did! He made me stop and think, and I knew I ought to ask you first."

"Good for you, Peter!" said Mum, and gave him a quick hug.

"But don't tell the others, please," begged Peter. "You see, Jesus has planted my seed, but I'm afraid it isn't very big yet."

"Keep on watering it with prayer," Mum reminded him.

5

Third Seed—Caroline

HAROLD was much nicer when he came to play with the children next day. They were busy building a sand-castle, and this time he didn't call sand-castles "sissy". Instead he set to work to help them with his fine big spade.

With four of them helping they were able to make a truly magnificent castle. It had a moat all round it, and four turrets made with pailfuls of sand at each corner. Peter, Caroline, Harold and Jennifer each took charge of one side. Harold made windows in his—to shoot arrows through, he said. Caroline decorated her side with shells. Peter made a flat space between the castle and the moat. He said it was for the soldiers to drill on.

Jennifer found a flat piece of wood and made a bridge. It had strings of bootlace seaweed to pull it up by if an enemy tried to get across. The others all came to admire it.

"That's super!" cried Harold. "Good enough to walk across!" He lifted his foot as if he were going to tread on the bridge.

"Don't!" begged Jennifer. "It's only strong enough for pretend people!"

I don't think Harold meant to tread on the bridge. But somehow or other his other foot slipped, and he came down on it, breaking it to bits!

Jennifer was so sorry she wanted to cry. She did manage to choke the sobs down, but she couldn't help two big tears coming into her eyes. Caroline saw them.

Now Caroline couldn't bear anyone to

"You hateful, wicked, cruel boy!"
she screamed

hurt her little sister, and she thought
Harold had done it on purpose. She lost
her temper.

"You hateful, wicked, cruel boy!" she

screamed, and she would have hit Harold with her spade if Peter hadn't caught hold of her arm. And then she turned round and hit Peter!

Peter tumbled down. Unluckily one of the buckets was just behind him, and he knocked his head on it, hard.

Caroline's rage went in a second. "Oh Peter," she cried, "I didn't mean to!" But Peter didn't answer, and lay quite still. His face went very white.

Caroline began to scream, "I've killed Peter! I've killed Peter!"

Harold said rather shakily, "I think he's only fainted. I fainted once when I fell out of my swing. They dabbed my face with cold water."

Jennifer choked her tears back, and went to fetch water from the pool. Mum was in the bungalow, so Caroline, crying bitterly, hurried as fast as she could through the dry slippery sand to fetch her. Harold and Jennifer sopped their hankies in the salt water and dabbed Peter's face.

Peter opened his eyes. "What are you doing that for?" he asked. "I washed my face this morning!" He tried to sit up. "Ow!" he said. "My head feels all funny."

Jennifer sat down and took his head on her lap. "You fell over and hit your head on that bucket," she told him. "It's bleeding a little."

"I'd lie quiet till your mum comes, if I were you," said Harold.

Jennifer wiped the cut with her hankie. The salt water stung, and Peter said "Ow!" again; but the colour was coming back into his face and he looked much better.

Then Mum came running, with Caroline. Caroline was still crying and saying, "I didn't mean to! I didn't mean to!"

Poor Mum, she did look worried. But when she had looked at Peter's head she smiled. "Cheer up!" she said. "It isn't very bad. We'll put a piece of plaster on it, and then I think he had better lie down for a while. Come along, my wounded soldier."

The cut was cleaned and strapped

Peter's head still felt funny, so he didn't mind Mum carrying him to the bungalow. The cut was cleaned and strapped, and then he was glad to lie on his bed.

"Now," said Mum to Caroline, "tell me just what happened."

"It was really my fault," said Harold quickly. "I trod on Jennifer's bridge. But honestly I didn't mean to. My foot slipped."

"No," said Caroline bravely, "it was my fault, because I lost my temper. I was going to hit Harold, but Peter stopped me, and I hit him instead."

"If the bucket hadn't been there Peter wouldn't have been much hurt," said Jennifer.

Caroline shook her head. "I'm just awful," she wailed. "When I lose my temper I don't have time to think. I'll do something wicked one day, I know I shall. What shall I do? Whatever shall I do?"

"The first thing," said Mum, "is to be quiet and let Peter rest."

"May I sit by him?" Caroline asked. "I'll be mousey quiet and not talk a word. Promise."

"Very well," agreed Mum. "The rest of us will go outside, because the Blob doesn't understand about keeping quiet! Would you like me to read you a story? Caroline can call us if Peter wants anything."

So Mum and the others went and sat on the sandhills and Mum read to them.

Caroline sat very still, watching Peter, who was feeling sleepy. She felt so miserable that the tears kept running down her cheeks, but she didn't make any noise. Presently Peter opened his eyes.

"Poor old Caro!" he whispered. "I know just how you feel. I felt like that about the Blob. I say, shall I tell you a secret?"

Caroline nodded.

Caroline sat very still, watching Peter

"You know," Peter went on, "we do mean to be good, but then something happens and we forget. We can't be good all by ourselves—see?"

Caroline nodded again.

"I asked Jesus to plant a seed of remembering in my heart, and He did. He reminded me not to go sailing with Harold without asking Mum first. Only you have to keep watering the seed.

That's praying." Peter was getting very sleepy. He yawned and then smiled at Caroline. "You try it," he said. "Ask Jesus. He'll help you." And then he went fast asleep.

Caroline sat and thought. Then she got off her chair and knelt down.

"Please, Jesus," she prayed, "plant a seed in me of keeping my temper. I can't be good without You! Jesus, help me."

When Mum came to peep into Peter's room, she found Peter asleep on his bed, and Caroline asleep on the floor. From the way she was lying all doubled up, Mum guessed she had been on her knees.

6

What Dad Saw

PETER was all right next day, except for a sore place on his head. This was a good thing, because it was Saturday, and Dad was coming for the week-end.

Mum drove them to meet him at the station. Peter sat in front, while Caroline and Jennifer sat behind with the Blob between them, trying to keep him from sliding off on to the floor. The Blob loved riding in a car.

It was not a very good day for the shore, as the tide was high, and there was only the strip of dry sand under the dunes. Besides, it was windy, and the sand kept blowing into their eyes. But as they drove Mum told them of a lovely plan she had made for the afternoon— they would all drive to the river and picnic there.

It was good to have Dad with them! He drove them back, the Blob sitting on Mum's knee and the three children squeezed into the back of the car, and everybody talked at once. After lunch they packed the picnic basket into the boot, and off they went. Mum had chosen a perfect place for tea, on a flat piece of grass by the river with a bank behind it which kept off the wind. Trees and bushes grew on the bank. One oak tree was so big and old that it had a hollow inside like a tiny room.

Mum spread the rug and she and Dad unpacked the picnic. Mum had made some long reins which she fastened round the Blob to keep him from crawling off and tumbling into the water.

"Now," said Dad, "if you kids will go

Mum spread the rug, and she and Dad
unpacked the picnic

and collect some dry sticks I will make a fire to boil the kettle on."

Dad was clever at making fires. With his pocket-knife he cut out a square of grass, roots and all, and put it on one side. He did this so that when the fire was done with he could cover up the black patch where it had been, and so not spoil their pretty picnic place. Then he and Mum sat talking while they waited for the children to bring sticks for the fire.

Peter came first. Dad saw him trotting along, carrying his bundle of sticks on his head. When he came to the hollow tree he stopped and smiled a twinkly smile to himself. Then he put down his sticks and crept right inside the tree.

"I hope he doesn't mean to play one of his silly tricks," said Dad.

Next came Jennifer. She was carrying her sticks in her arms, and one of them was so long that she had to be careful not to trip over it.

Peter, inside the tree, made a funny little noise, "Bom-bom! Bom-bom!"

Jennifer stopped, and her eyes opened
very wide

"Now Jennifer will be frightened," thought Dad. Jennifer stopped, and her eyes opened very wide. Then she saw Peter's bundle of sticks under the tree, and she laughed.

"I know you, old Peter!" she cried, and Peter poked his head out, grinning.

"Good old Jennifer!" he said. "I didn't scare you, did I? I only made a very little noise, on purpose."

"Peter's getting some sense at last," Dad said to Mum.

"No," said Jennifer, "I wasn't frightened—except just for one second I wondered what it was. Then I knew it was you."

"Come inside," said Peter, "and bring that nice long stick of yours. We'll see if we can make Caroline jump."

Jennifer crawled into the tree. Presently Caroline came along singing to herself, with her sticks under her arm. Peter let her just get by, then he reached out with the long stick and tickled the back of her legs. Caroline did jump! Right up into the air like a rabbit. She whirled round to see what had touched her. When she heard Peter chuckle her face got very red and her eyes had that sparkly look they got when she was angry.

"Now for one of Caroline's rages," sighed Dad.

But Caroline shut her mouth tightly and stood still. The sparkle went out of her eyes. Then she burst out laughing.

"You just come out of there, Peter!" she cried. "I'll teach you to tickle people when they aren't looking."

"Well, wonders will never cease!" remarked Dad.

Out came Peter, and out came Jennifer, and all three of them laughed and laughed. Caroline threw down her sticks and they all caught hands and danced round and round in a ring.

"The seeds are growing!" sang Caroline. "I didn't get angry!"

"The seeds are growing!" sang Peter. "I did remember!"

"The seeds are growing!" sang Jennifer. "I wasn't afraid!"

"Hi, you kids!" called out Dad. "What about the fire for our tea? And what's all this about seeds?"

The three children gathered up their sticks and walked over to Mum and Dad.

"It's a secret really," Peter said.

"Mum knows about it, though," said Jennifer.

"And of course we'll tell *you*," added Caroline.

"I'm just longing to hear," said Dad, "but keep it until I've got the fire going."

So, when Dad had lit a bright little fire and Mum had balanced the kettle on two logs, they all cuddled up to Dad and explained. When they had finished Dad put his arms round all three of them at once and hugged.

"That's the best news I ever heard in all my life!" he said.

Mum smiled all over her dear face, and the Blob said "Gug-gug-gug—bvah!" as if he understood. Of course he didn't!

"When the Blob is older we'll tell him too," said Jennifer.

Then the kettle boiled and they all had tea.

I can't honestly say that Peter and Caroline and Jennifer were always sensible and patient and brave for the rest of their lives. Things don't happen like that, and all of them had to do a lot of watering before their seeds grew into strong tall plants of thoughtfulness and good temper and courage. But Jesus never lets anyone down who truly wants His help.

Do you know what He said about seeds growing secretly? Ask someone to show you the place in the Bible.